Give your child a he
PICTURE RE

Dear Parent,

Now children as young as preschool age can have the fun and satisfaction of reading a book all on their own.

In every Picture Reader, there are simple words, rebus pictures, and 24 flash cards to cut out and keep. (There is a flash card for every rebus picture plus extra cards for reading practice.) After children listen to each story a couple of times, they will be ready to try it all by themselves.

Collect all the titles in our Picture Reader series. Once children have mastered these books, they can move on to Levels 1, 2, and 3 in our All Aboard Reading series.

For Gussie and Millie—M.A.H.

 Published by Grosset & Dunlap, Inc., a member of Penguin Putnam Books for Young Readers, New York. ALL ABOARD READING is a trademark of The Putnam & Grosset Group. GROSSET & DUNLAP is a trademark of Grosset & Dunlap, Inc. Published simultaneously in Canada. Printed in the U.S.A. Library of Congress Catalog Card Number: 97-78301

ISBN 0-448-41849-5 A B C D E F G H I J

A PICTURE READER

Is That You, Santa?

By Margaret A. Hartelius

Grosset & Dunlap • New York

It is Christmas Eve.

The  is trimmed.

The  are hung.

 for are

on the 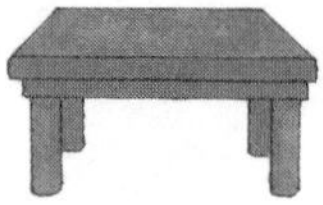 .

Daddy says,

"Now, it is time for 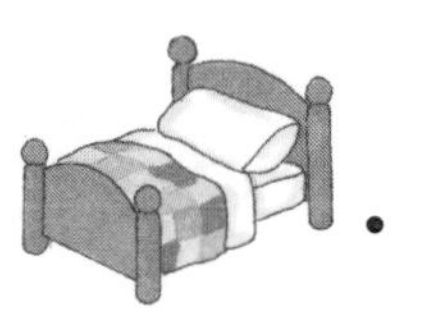.

 is coming soon."

Ring-a-ding-ding!

I hear !

It must be 

with his 

and his 

filled with toys!

"Is that you, ?"

"No!" says Mommy.

"It's just the .

Go back to 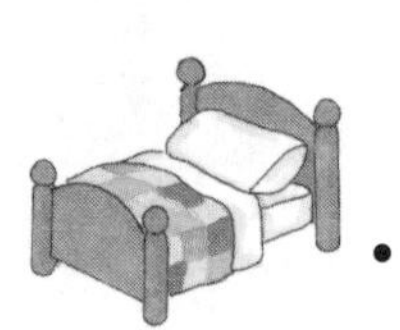."

YELLOW PAGES

Whoosh! Bang!

What was that?

I know. It's !

He is coming

down our 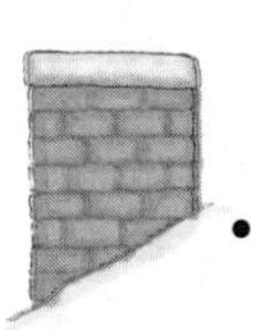.

"Is that you, 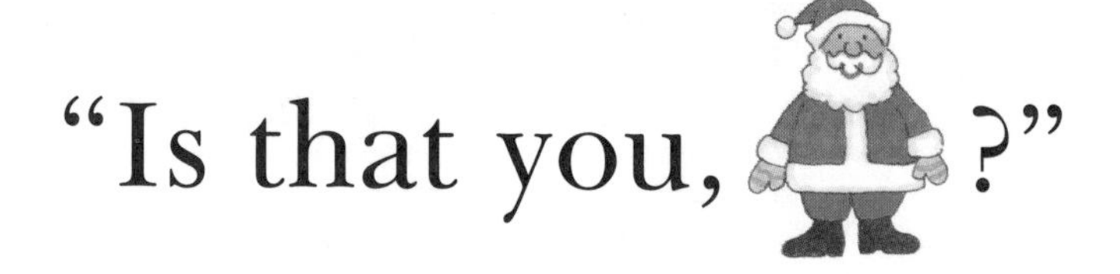?"

"No!" says Daddy.

"I took out the trash.

The wind blew

the 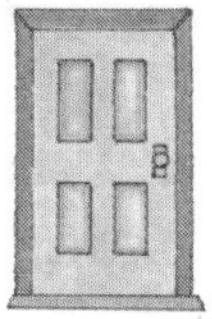 shut.

Go back to ."

Crack! Crash!

Hear that?

It must be .

 is putting

the BIG 

under the !

And he broke

some of the .

"Is that you,  ?"

"No!" says Mommy.

"It is the  .

She was under the .

She broke some .

Go back to ."

Munch, munch!

 is eating the !

"Ho! Ho! Ho!"

says .

He likes our .

 is here!

"Is that you, ?"

No! It's Mommy and

Daddy eating 

and watching .

Mommy says,

"GO TO 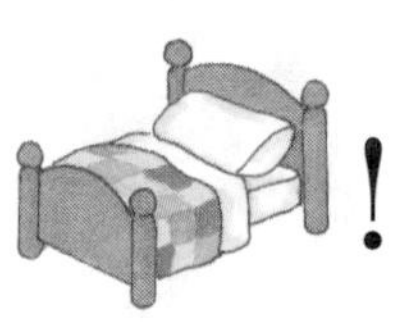!

 will not come

if you are not in ."

I go to .

I wait and wait.

But no .

I am getting sleepy.

My are closing.

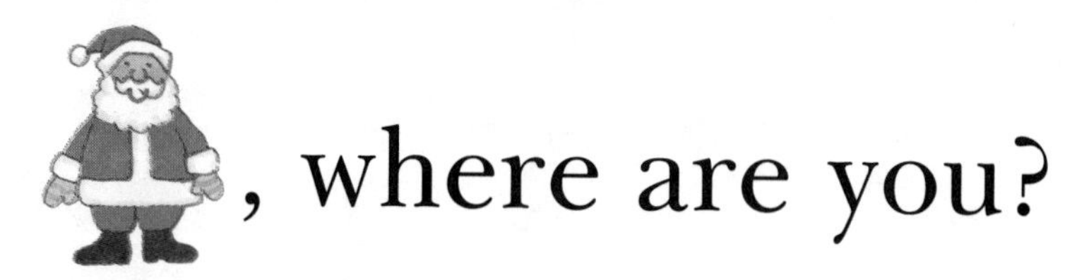, where are you?

Sh-h-h! Here I am!

Look at all the  !

 did come!

But, I did not hear  .

How did he do that?

CUT OUT FLASH CARDS ALONG DOTTED LINES.

cookies	tree
Santa	stockings
bed	table

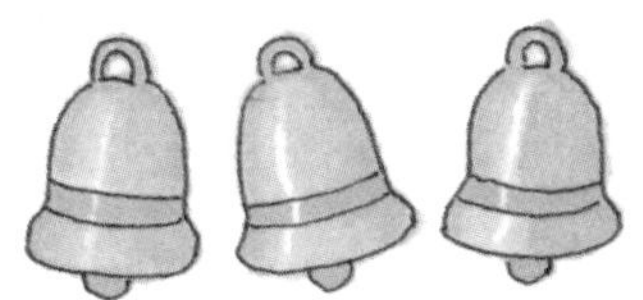

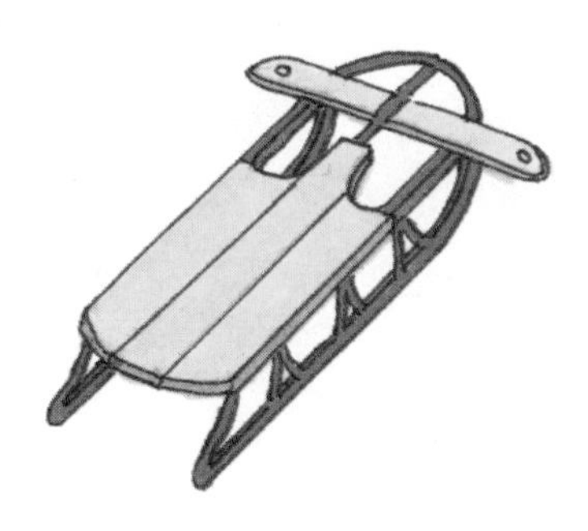

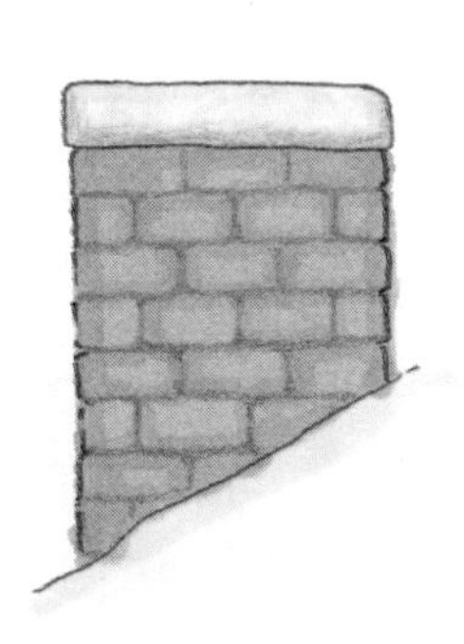

CUT OUT FLASH CARDS ALONG DOTTED LINES.

reindeer

bells

telephone

sled

door

chimney

bike	fireplace
bear	TV
presents	boots

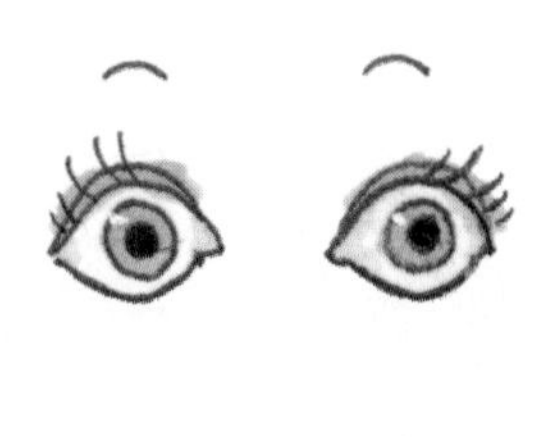

CUT OUT EACH CARD ALONG DOTTED LINES.

balls	stairs
popcorn	cat
candles	eyes